When You Were a Baby

By Katharine Ross

Photographs by Phoebe Dunn

Learning Ladders/Random House

Text copyright © 1988 by Random House, Inc. Photographs copyright © 1988 by Phoebe Dunn.
All rights reserved under International and Pan-American Copyright Conventions.
Published in the United States by Random House, Inc., New York, and simultaneously
in Canada by Random House of Canada Limited, Toronto.

Library of Congress Cataloging-in-Publication Data:
Ross, Katharine, 1950–
When you were a baby / Katharine Ross ; photographs by Phoebe Dunn. p. cm.
SUMMARY: A parent describes for a child all the things experienced in babyhood,
from the first perceptions of sight and sound to the beginning of
crawling and walking. ISBN: 0-394-89897-4 (trade); 0-394-99897-9 (lib. bdg.)
[1. Babies—Fiction.] I. Dunn, Phoebe, ill. II. Title.
PZ7.R719693Wh 1988 [E]—dc19 87-37464

Manufactured in the United States of America 1 2 3 4 5 6 7 8 9 0

When you were a baby, at first you didn't do much of anything.

You slept.

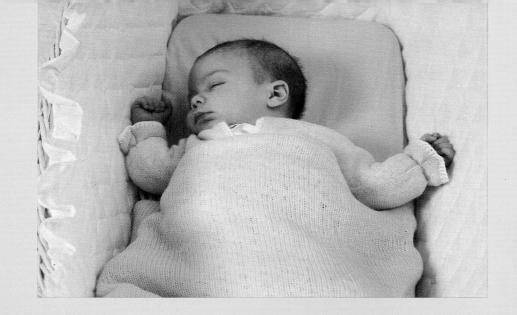

You cried.

When you were very new, we didn't know why you were crying. Then we learned to tell the wet cry from the tired cry from the hungry cry. Mostly, you were hungry.

You ate…   and ate.

And then you slept some more.

You couldn't see very well at first.
But you could hear things.

You heard cars going past outside.

You heard someone playing the piano.

You heard dogs barking.

Sometimes, sudden loud noises
startled you and you burst into tears.

Other times, soft music lulled
you to sleep.

Every day we took you outside for fresh air.

You lay in the carriage and stared up at the sky and trees. People leaned down and told you what a beautiful baby you were.

And when we took you out for a walk in the backpack, you nearly always fell fast asleep.

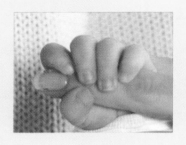

We held out our fingers to you. You grabbed them and gripped them tightly. For such a tiny baby, you were very strong!

Your neck got stronger and so did your back. You didn't know it then, but you were exercising all the time. When we put you on your tummy, you held your head up, each day a little higher and a little steadier…and you smiled.

You were so proud of yourself! And so were we.

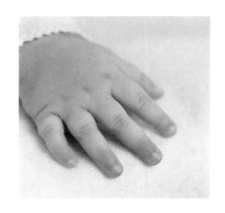

You discovered an amazing new toy: your hands.

And with that toy, you discovered yet another toy: your toes. Hello, toes!

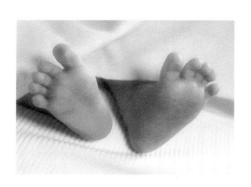

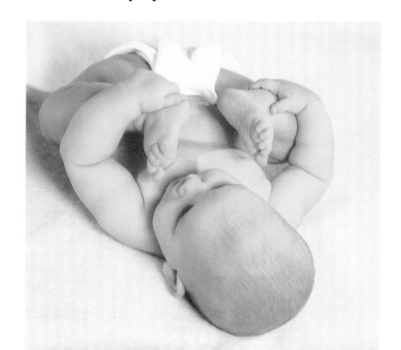

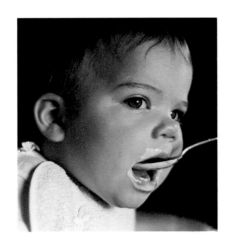

You tasted your first real food. Yum.
Rice cereal … then yogurt. We fed
you a different kind of food every week.

First we fed you, then you took the spoon
and fed yourself.

But nothing tasted quite so good as
finger food.

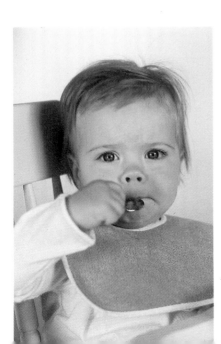

You smiled all the time now. But no one could make you smile quicker than an older child.

We played pat-a-cake, and that was fun.

You made faces at yourself in the mirror, and that was fun too.

Then you started teething—
and that was no fun at all!
You sucked on your fist and
you fretted.

Sometimes you were so
uncomfortable you couldn't
eat and you couldn't sleep.
Nothing helped.

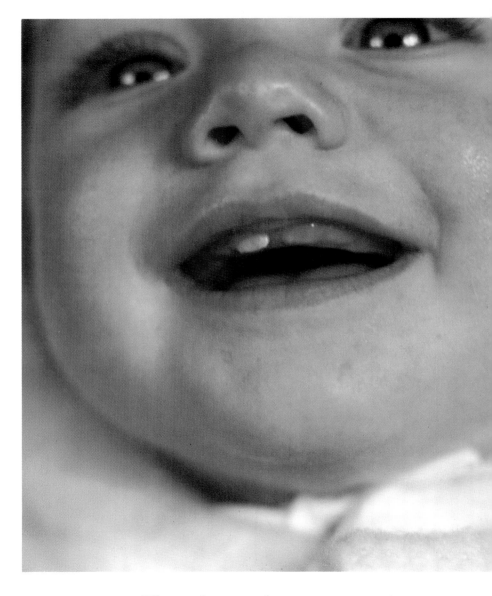

Then the tooth came in and
everything was sunny again!

With a little help, you could sit up.
Upsy-daisy!

And before long, you were sitting
up all by yourself, looking at books,
playing with toys, and visiting
with friends.

But your favorite time of day was bathtime.

You slapped the water with your hand and made a splash. You squeezed the washcloth and stared at the bubbles.

Afterward, we dried you with a soft, fluffy towel and gave you lots of hugs and kisses. How clean and fresh you smelled after your bath!

You were still busy with those back-strengthening exercises. By now, you were pushing yourself up on your hands and knees and rocking back and forth.

Then one day, you put it all together and began to crawl. Crawling was fantastic. Now you could crawl over to all those mysterious things you used to stare at from our arms, and touch and hold and study them up close.

As a crawler, you were busier than ever. Looking under things ...

even pulling yourself up to a stand to look on top of things. There was no end to your curiosity!

When the weather grew warm, we took
you outside and you explored nature.
You touched flowers…
and animals…
and leaves.

"Be gentle now," we told you when you met a bunny rabbit
for the first time.

Every time we turned around, you were pulling yourself up to a stand.

Then one day, you took your first few steps. You were a little wobbly at first ... but so pleased with yourself.

And before we knew it, you were toddling all over the place, discovering what you had known all along: that the world is a wonderful and fascinating place to live in.

And suddenly, you weren't a baby anymore!